PUFFIN BOOKS

HAPPY HOLIDAY, HAMMY THE WONDER HAMSTER

Hamilton ran along Bethany's bookshelves until he found a book called *Sea and Shore – the Life of the British Coastline. With such a boring title,* Hamilton thought, *it deserves to be eaten by a hamster.* All the same, he pulled it from the shelf, turned the pages and saw . . .

. . . sand. And more sand. Pale sand, dark sand, sand with ripples where the waves had been. Deep, soft sand.

He closed his eyes to imagine it. The thought of all that trickly, grainy, yellow sand made his head spin. When Bethany came back, he tapped the book with his claws and looked up at her.

'Yes,' she said, turning the pages. 'Yes, that's the seaside.'

Hamilton held out his paw for her mobile phone

HOW

Have you read all of Hammy's adventures?

HAMMY THE WONDER HAMSTER

HAPPY CHRISTMAS, HAMMY THE WONDER HAMSTER

HAPPY HOLIDAY, HAMMY THE WONDER HAMSTER!

POPPY HARRIS

HAPPY HOLIDAY, HAMMY THE WONDER HAMSTER

PUFFIN

PUFFIN BOOKS

Published by the Penguin Group
Penguin Books Ltd, 80 Strand, London WC2R ORL, England
Penguin Group (USA) Inc., 375 Hudson Street, New York, New York 10014, USA
Penguin Group (Canada), 90 Eglinton Avenue East, Suite 700, Toronto, Ontario, Canada M4P 2Y3
(a division of Pearson Penguin Canada Inc.)
Penguin Ireland, 25 St Stephen's Green, Dublin 2, Ireland (a division of Penguin Books Ltd)
Penguin Group (Australia), 250 Camberwell Road, Camberwell, Victoria 3124, Australia
(a division of Pearson Australia Group Pty Ltd)
Penguin Books India Pvt Ltd, 11 Community Centre, Panchsheel Park, New Delhi – 110 017, India
Penguin Group (NZ), 67 Apollo Drive, Rosedale, North Shore 0632, New Zealand
(a division of Pearson New Zealand Ltd)
Penguin Books (South Africa) (Pty) Ltd, 24 Sturdee Avenue, Rosebank, Johannesburg 2196, South Africa

Penguin Books Ltd, Registered Offices: 80 Strand, London WC2R ORL, England

puffinbooks.com

First published 2010
1

Text copyright © Poppy Harris, 2010
Illustrations copyright © Dan Bramall, 2010
All rights reserved

The moral right of the author and illustrator has been asserted

Set in 13.75/20.5pt Bembo
Typeset by Palimpsest Book Production Limited, Grangemouth, Stirlingshire
Made and printed in England by Clays Ltd, St Ives plc

British Library Cataloguing in Publication Data
A CIP catalogue record for this book is available from the British Library

ISBN: 978-0-141-32486-9

www.greenpenguin.co.uk

Penguin Books is committed to a sustainable future
for our business, our readers and our planet.
The book in your hands is made from paper
certified by the Forest Stewardship Council.

To Bracha and Tovi

chapter 1

Hamilton the hamster was very fond of his
human friend Bethany. She looked after him,
played with him and chatted to him, but today
she puzzled him.

Hamilton wasn't easily puzzled. He was an
amazingly intelligent hamster, who could do
crosswords and Sudoku in his head and loved
helping Bethany with her homework. This
morning he had just woken up from a lovely
dream about running for miles in hot desert
sand, and all he could see of Bethany was her

feet, which were sticking out from under her bed. Why was she crawling about under there? He gnawed on a wooden clothes peg, which was his favourite thing today, and watched until she crawled out backwards, pulling her backpack out with her. Then he scratched at the bars of his cage.

'Oh, hello!' said Bethany, pushing trails of dark hair out of her eyes. 'You've woken up!'

Hamilton put his head on one side and looked hard at the backpack. It was the summer holidays, so Bethany didn't need it for school.

'Do you want to know why I need this?' she asked. 'I was going to tell you, but you were asleep.'

She would have opened Hamilton's cage, but he was already doing that himself. He stepped on to her outstretched hand and sat up to listen as she stroked his soft white and gold fur.

'Nan and Grandie – that's Mum's parents – live at Kettle Bay,' said Bethany, 'by the seaside, and, Hamilton, it's just *fantastic* there. You can get straight down to the beach from their house – it's so close – and it's one of my favourite places ever. And they've invited Sam and me to go there to stay, all next week!'

Hamilton didn't see what was so good about this. Bethany was going away?

'Now, Hamilton,' she went on, 'Mum said she'd look after you, and so did Chloe, but I don't want to leave you. Would you like to come on holiday with me to the seaside?'

Hamilton tipped his head to one side to think about it.

'Mum might be a bit difficult about it, but she'll get used to the idea,' said Bethany. 'So what do you think? Do you want to come on holiday with me?'

Rain began to patter on the window and

Mum's voice called from downstairs: 'Bethany! Sam! Come and help me bring the washing in!'

'I have to go,' said Bethany. 'Have a think about what I said. And –' she placed a neatly cut-out square of newspaper in front of him – 'there's your crossword.'

Hamilton usually did the crossword as soon as Bethany gave it to him, but today she had asked him to think about going on holiday, so he left the crossword for a little bit and did think, very hard. He was astonishingly good at that.

Hamilton didn't know why he was so brainy. Neither did Bethany. There was one person who did, and his name was Dr Tim Taverner.

Tim Taverner worked at the university in the nearest town. He was doing some very secret (and illegal) work and had made a microchip packed with artificial intelligence. It was so small it was really only a microspeck, but one dreadful morning he had accidently brushed it into his waste-paper basket along with some sesame seeds, crumbs, bits of apple and a paper aeroplane (making paper planes helped him to concentrate). By the time he realized what he'd done, Mary the cleaner had emptied the bins, shredded the paper and taken it all to Dolittle's Pet Shop to be used as bedding in the hamster cages. Until then, Hamilton had only been a young gold-and-white hamster waiting for somebody to buy him, but when he nibbled at that paper, the microspeck had become stuck in his cheek pouch. It was still there, firmly embedded.

Hamilton didn't know about the microspeck in his cheek. He only knew that he loved reading and puzzles, maths, engineering, apples and aeroplanes – and that Bethany was the nicest person in the world.

What Hamilton — and Bethany — *did* know was that it was very important to keep Hamilton's great intelligence a secret between the two of them. Bethany knew that if other people found out about it there would be a fuss, with newspaper reporters and television cameras, and sooner or later somebody important would take Hamilton away from her and make him do intelligence tests and have brain scans. She and Hamilton didn't want any of this to happen, so nobody else knew his secret. Not even Chloe.

Hamilton considered what Bethany had said about a holiday. He'd be bored without her. Chloe was very nice, but she was always calling him Hammy (which was bearable) or Fluffpot (which he hated). Chloe's hamster, Toffee, would be in his own cage, so he wouldn't do Hamilton any harm, but he was a bit dim and you couldn't have a decent conversation with him. An afternoon at Chloe's was all right, but Hamilton didn't want to go there for a whole week.

The only trouble with going to the seaside, Hamilton decided, was the sea. He knew he wasn't supposed to get wet, but being a brave, inquisitive hamster, he was always having adventures, and some of them had turned out to be wet adventures and a danger to his health. Being a wet hamster was not pleasant. He certainly didn't want to go into the sea, and didn't think Bethany should either. But where there was sea there was a beach, and where there was a beach there was . . .

He shivered with delight at the thought of it . . .

Sand!

Hamilton had never touched sand, but he knew that hamsters are originally desert animals

7

and the idea of sand fascinated him. He needed to find out more about beaches. His favourite way of finding things out was on the Internet, but he couldn't use the computer today, when Mum and Bethany's little brother Sam were around. Pity about that.

Hamilton ran along Bethany's bookshelves until he found a book called *Sea and Shore – the Life of the British Coastline. With such a boring title*, Hamilton thought, *it deserves to be eaten by a hamster.* All the same, he pulled it from the shelf, turned the pages and saw . . .

. . . sand. And more sand. Pale sand, dark sand, sand with ripples where the waves had been. Deep, soft sand.

He closed his eyes to imagine it. The thought of all that trickly, grainy, yellow sand made his head spin. When Bethany came back, he tapped the book with his claws and looked up at her.

'Yes,' she said, turning the pages. 'Yes, that's the seaside.'

Hamilton held out his paw for her mobile phone and tapped out a message.

HOW SOON CAN WE GO THERE?

chapter 2

Mum and Dad couldn't see why Bethany needed to take her hamster on holiday and told her he'd be happier at home. Bethany knew perfectly well that he wouldn't. But she couldn't tell them that she and her hamster had already discussed it.

'He'll miss me,' she said. 'He'll pine for me.'

'It's only a week,' said Mum, 'and you can't expect Nan and Grandie to put up with a hamster as well as you and Sam.'

'Why not?' asked Bethany, and before they

could think of an answer she added, 'I'll be looking after him, and he's no trouble, Mum. You and Auntie Sally had guinea-pigs when you lived there, and they never minded that.'

'That was different,' said Mum.

'What sort of different?' demanded Bethany.

Mum sighed. 'Different because we were their children, not their grandchildren, and besides, Nan and Grandie were younger then,' she said. That didn't make any sense to Bethany.

'The change might not be good for Hamilton,' Dad pointed out. 'It might make him ill. Hamsters are delicate.'

'I know that!' she said, trying not to sound cross because that would make things worse. Bethany resented the idea that she wouldn't know what was best for Hamilton. But there was no point in making a fight of it, so she just shrugged.

'I'm going to clean out his cage,' she announced calmly, and left. Bethany was good at quietly holding out for her own way. Patience usually worked.

It worked this time, too. When the phone rang next day, Bethany answered it. It was, as she had hoped, Grandie.

'We're looking forward to having you two next week!' said Grandie. 'Your Nan's already filling up the freezer with cake.'

'We're looking forward to it, too,' said Bethany. 'Grandie, please – can I ask you something?'

'You can ask me anything, sweetheart!' said Grandie.

'It's about Hamilton, my hamster,' she said. 'I don't want to leave him behind. He might miss me and go off his food, and he's never any trouble, so, will it be all right if I bring him with me?'

'Oh, I do hope you will!' said Grandie. 'Your mum and Auntie Sally kept guinea-pigs, you know. It's a long time since we had a little animal in the house! Will you let me hold him?'

So that was that. On Friday evening, Bethany packed some clothes, including lots of T-shirts, sandals, her swimming costume (blue-and-green and very new), sun block, toothpaste, toothbrush, hairbrush, plenty of good books, her sketch book and some apples to share with Hamilton. In a separate bag, she put hamster food, raisins, some Sudoku puzzles from the Internet, a wooden clothes peg for Hamilton to chew and the cardboard tube from a kitchen roll so he had a tunnel to play in.

While Bethany was busy packing for both of them, Hamilton let himself out of his cage and ran downstairs. He found an open window, jumped out and, keeping a sharp eye open for cats, ran to the garden shed where he squeezed under the door. Bobby the bunny, who belonged to Sam, was sitting in his cage eating a carrot.

'Hello, Bobby!' said Hamilton, who spoke Rabbit perfectly. 'How are you this evening?'

'Oh, it's you,' said Bobby with his mouth full. He looked down at the unfinished food in his bowl. 'Want a carrot?'

'No thank you,' said Hamilton quickly. He didn't want to eat food that had been lying in Bobby's dish. Besides, he knew that Bobby was only being polite and really wanted to eat the carrots himself.

'Did you know your Sam's going on holiday tomorrow?' asked Hamilton.

'Yeah,' said Bobby without looking up. 'He told me. He said his mum and dad will feed me and keep me clean, so I'm not bothered.'

'Not bothered?' said Hamilton, who found this hard to understand. 'Because, if you do

14

want to come, I'm sure I can get Bethany to talk to Sam and they'll arrange it all.'

Bobby was so surprised that he stopped eating. 'What would I want to go for?' he asked. 'I'm warm here. I'm fed. I've got a run so I can play on the lawn and eat it. I'm not going anywhere.'

Hamilton gave up and went back to Bethany, who was squeezing a packet of mints into a corner of her bag.

'I won't sleep tonight,' she said as he ran on to her knee. 'I'll be too excited. Now, Hamilton, there are things you need to know about the seaside. It's colder than the desert, for a start. Always stay close to me, and remember that the tide comes in very quickly, so stay away from the shoreline. If you burrow too deep, you'll find that the sand gets damp.'

Hamilton wrinkled his nose at her. Bethany laughed.

'Yes, I know,' she said. 'You think I don't have to tell you all this, but I do. I've been to the beach before and I know what it's like, so I have to warn you.'

Hamilton reached out a paw to ask for her phone, tapped out a message then handed the phone back. She read it and laughed again.

'Yes, I know I'm being fussy,' she said. 'That's because you keep getting into danger – and I don't want you to be harmed.'

BUT IT'S ALWAYS OK IN THE END, he texted.

However, that wasn't the point, and Hamilton knew it. Bethany looked at him sternly. But it's hard to be stern with a very fluffy hamster who's teasing you, so she laughed.

'All the same, Hamilton,' she said, 'I get very worried about you when I can't find you, and very *very* worried when you get wet. You were

16

lucky to survive at Christmas, running out into the snow like that. I thought I'd never see you alive again!'

Hamilton felt sorry immediately. He didn't mean to worry Bethany. He ran up her arm and nuzzled against her cheek to tell her that he didn't mean to upset her, and he really was very fond of her, and all those things that people say with a hug and intelligent hamsters say with a nuzzle. So long as he did what Bethany said, he'd be perfectly safe, unless . . .

He ran to the phone again and asked, R THERE ANY CATS AT THE CSIDE?

'I've never seen one at Kettle Bay,' said Bethany.

There you are then, thought Hamilton. *No problem!*

chapter 3

Bethany was woken next morning by Sam jumping on to her bed.

'Yay!' he was shouting. 'It's sunny! Get up!'

Bethany grabbed at the duvet as he tried to pull it off her, and sleepily curled up again. Eventually she got up and dressed, and was ready and impatient for Mum to drive them to Kettle Bay. But even so, it seemed a lifetime before they reached the seaside. Before they could set off, there were still frisbees and Sam's cricket stuff to pack, and Mum kept remembering things like wellies and insect repellent. Bethany thought they'd never get away. After that, it still took over an hour to drive there. In his cage, Hamilton stood up on his hind legs, straining to look out of the windows, yet in spite of the excitement he did find he was falling asleep. He couldn't help it. He'd been up all night running on his wheel and pretending to be in the desert.

Even when they got to Kettle Bay, it still seemed to take forever before anyone got to the beach. First, Nan said they should all have lunch together before Mum went home, so Hamilton decided he might as well have another sleep. Then, when he woke up, half the things that had just been packed into the boot were being packed again into a bag for Nan to take to the beach. Why couldn't people have cheek pouches, like sensible animals? Finally, Nan told Bethany all the important things that Bethany already knew by heart, which were:

Stay where we can see you.

Paddle in the shallows but don't swim, because there are strong currents further out.

Always take your phone.

While all this was happening, Bethany glanced down and saw Hamilton in his cage, watching and listening with a twinkle in his eye. *Yes, I know*, she thought as he winked at her, *this is just the way I talked to you*. Bethany didn't ask for permission to take Hamilton with her to the beach – even Nan and Grandie wouldn't have let her do that – but when she took his cage upstairs, she secretly popped Hamilton into her bag with her phone and a packet of tissues.

Nan, Grandie, Sam, Bethany and a hidden Hamilton finally made it out into the sunshine. There was a taste of salty freshness on the

breeze, and Bethany could see the rippling
blue-grey and sparkle of the sea, and the wide,
everlasting stretch of sky and water. Sand dunes,
those small, firm, sandy mounds with spiky
grass (the kind you don't touch because it can
cut your fingers), led on to an arc of golden
and inviting sandy beach. Bethany took off her
sandals and sank her feet into the kind, warm
sand. The tide was out and the shoreline was
firm and golden. Little white shells and pebbles
washed smooth by the sea lay in wavy lines
where the sea had left them.

The bay curved round in a broad semicircle
like a protecting arm. To the left and right
stretched the flat rocks, and Bethany knew that
the tide would have left rock pools full of small,
ferny plants, delicate little seaweeds, limpets and
the funny, inquisitive hermit crabs in their
shells. At the edge of the rocks was a very
brightly painted pole with a lifebelt attached,

for throwing to anyone who might be in difficulty in the water. Bethany always thought lifebelts looked like big red-and-white doughnuts. She slipped her hand into her bag, where Hamilton was staying very still, and stroked the top of his head to reassure him.

Hamilton was clinging on with all his front claws to the inside of that bag. He could smell the warm, dry sand, and the urge to leap from Bethany's bag and dig himself into it was almost overwhelming.

'Grandie, can we play cricket?' asked Sam.

'Course we can!' said Grandie, and they ran down to the firm sand nearest to the waves. Nan sighed and said she supposed she'd have to join in, but they all knew she actually loved playing cricket on the beach.

'I'll stay here and make a sandcastle,' said Bethany, and she knelt where the sand was dry and warm. As soon as the others were busy

with stumps and bales and talking about who
would bat first, she said quietly, 'Out you get,
Hamilton.'

Hamilton leapt from her pocket, dived head
first into the sand, and scrabbled. Soon only his
hind paws and fluffy little bottom were sticking
out, before they too vanished completely.
Bethany could only see where he was from the
shifting of the sand above him. At last,
Hamilton's pink nose popped out from a
mound, followed quickly by the rest of him.
He shook himself vigorously, scratched the sand
from his ears, rubbed his face, then threw
himself back on to the beach, rolling on his
back and kicking for joy. Bethany thought she'd
never seen him so happy.

'We're here for a whole week!' she told
Hamilton. 'If it stays sunny, and Nan says it
will, we can come here every day. I'm going to
build you a castle, but what we need to do first

is to find a stone, a special stone, one that looks different from the others. Stay there and don't move from that spot.'

Hamilton wriggled into a sand nest and watched Bethany inquisitively while she hunted among the pebbles on the shoreline. He couldn't imagine how a stone was going to add to the delight of sand burrowing. Bethany came back with a very pretty oval-shaped one, pink and grey and very smooth, quite unlike the others.

'This is our stone,' she said. 'If you go for a dig, leave it on the surface and stay near to it so I can always find you. If you move, move the stone too. That way, I'll always know where you are even when I can't see you.'

Hamilton was impressed. Bethany might not be good at maths, but in some ways she was even cleverer than he was! It must be a different kind of clever. He put the stone in his mouth, where it fitted neatly into one of his pouches, and helped Bethany to build her castle.

It was a real storybook castle, with a moat, a keep and turrets at the corners. Hamilton helped her to dig out the moat but then couldn't resist jumping on to the keep, which gave way underneath him. He held out his paw for the phone, but from the look on his face Bethany already knew what he wanted to say.

'I know you're sorry,' she said, laughing. 'It doesn't matter – I'll soon build it again!'

Hamilton scrabbled into the sand again, but just before he disappeared, he remembered the pebble, popped back up and left it as a marker for Bethany. This time, he was gone for several minutes, but he appeared again at last, wrinkling his nose and brushing sand from his whiskers.

'I told you it got damp further down,' said

Bethany. 'Perhaps you should stay near the surface . . . Oh! Hamilton! Hamilton, come and see what I've found!'

Hamilton sat up hopefully. Bethany sounded very excited. In stories, children found treasure maps near the sea. He knew this was unlikely, but a fossil or a previously unknown sort of shell would be good. He was disappointed to see that all Bethany was holding up was a small stick.

'People shouldn't throw lolly sticks away,' she said. 'It's litter. But they do make very good flags. Look – you take a bit of sweet wrapper or an old ticket or something, then you can push the lolly stick through it – like this – and there's a flag for your castle!'

She held out the flag to him. Hamilton pounced on it with both paws, held it high and waved it from side to side. Bethany was ready to laugh, but didn't because she knew that he was being a knight, or maybe a herald, and she didn't want to upset his dignity.

Hamilton was delighted with his flag. Not many things were hamster-sized, but this was, so he flourished it, held it high and finally scrambled up the sandcastle to plant it on a tower. The tower fell down, but Bethany quickly built it up again while he chewed at the lolly stick.

He was beginning to have a lot of respect for his hamster ancestors from the desert. Sand was wonderful but it was getting into Hamilton's mouth, his ears and his eyes too, if he wasn't careful. It was even between his teeth. He supposed those long-ago desert hamsters must have become used to it. Bethany didn't seem bothered by it at all. Perhaps she felt as he did – sand was so lovely that it didn't matter if it stuck to your claws and whiskers.

But afternoons on the beach don't last

forever, and when Bethany saw Nan, Grandie and Sam packing up the cricket things, she scooped up Hamilton and put him gently back in her bag.

'It looks as if we're going home soon,' she said. 'Stay there and keep still.'

Hamilton wasn't used to taking so much exercise at this time of day. He stretched, had another shake, settled down – and was deeply asleep by the time they all reached home. Upstairs in her room, Bethany placed him very gently in his nest box. He blinked a bit, yawned, decided not to wake up and was still fast asleep when Bethany came to bed.

chapter 4

Dr Tim Taverner had never given up his quest
to find the hamster with the microspeck. He
knew that it belonged either to Bethany or to
her friend Chloe, who lived in the same street,
Tumblers Crescent, with her hamster called
Toffee. Tim Taverner wanted that microspeck
back and was determined to get his hands on
the hamster. So far, all his attempts had failed,
but unbeknown to Bethany and Hamilton, he
wasn't going to stop trying.

The day after Bethany and Sam went to

Kettle Bay was a Sunday, so there was a lot of garden tidying and car washing going on, and Tim made a point of walking round Tumblers Crescent with a newspaper under his arm so as not to look too suspicious. When he heard two people talking, his ears pricked up. And when he realized that the voices were coming from Number 33, where Bethany lived, and that one of the speakers was Bethany's mum, he hurried over at once, accidentally on purpose dropping his newspaper and picking it up again so that he could stop and listen to them.

'Have the kids settled in all right with your mum and dad?' asked the woman next door.

'Oh, yes,' said Bethany's mum. 'Bethany rang last night and they're having a great time. The forecast for Kettle Bay is good for the rest of the week too, so they'll be on the beach every day.'

Tim pretended to be struggling to sort out his newspaper as he listened with growing excitement. If the girl they were talking about, Bethany, was the hamster's owner, this would be a great chance to steal it. Now that the child wasn't around to stand guard over her precious hamster, he could get into the house, snatch it from its cage and run for it.

In his pocket, Tim carried a tracking device which could detect the microspeck, and he knew it worked because it had brought him very near to the hamster before. It had been broken on his last failed attempt to steal the hamster, but he'd mended it now. He reached for the tracking device, stood up and began to walk slowly down the street towards the house. But, for some reason, the tracking device wasn't picking anything up. Where on earth was the hamster and – more importantly – Tim's microspeck?

'So I suppose you're looking after the pets?' asked the neighbour.

'Funnily enough, no,' said Bethany's mum.

Tim stopped. He took off his glasses and polished them on his tie.

'I've got Sam's rabbit to look after,' went on Bethany's mum, 'but Bethany took her hamster with her.'

'Oh, bless her!' said the neighbour.

'I wasn't keen on the idea,' admitted Mum, 'but my parents are happy with it, and you know what she's like about her Hamilton – she won't be parted from him!'

Tim put his glasses back on and continued walking down the street, so concerned to look innocent that he didn't see where he was going and walked into a lamp-post. But even that didn't spoil his excitement. So, if he'd got the right child, the hamster was on holiday at Kettle Bay!

When he had been a teenager, Tim had liked canoeing. He was sure Kettle Bay would be a nice place to start up his old hobby again. He hadn't done it for years, but his old canoe was still hanging from the ceiling of his parents' garage.

Tim didn't often go to see his mum and dad – he felt more at home with computers than with people – but that same day he fitted a roof-rack on to his car, drove to his parents' house and collected his canoe.

When he got it home, he saw how neglected it was. There were cracks here and there, but it seemed seaworthy enough. He'd go down to the DIY store and buy some Patching Up Your Canoe stuff and a new life-jacket. Oh, and some more batteries for the remote-control tracking device. *Nothing* was going to stop him this time.

By the time Tim went to bed that night, he

had booked the first room he could get, in a bed and breakfast called the Hammock and Spinnaker.

He would stay at Kettle Bay as long as he needed to.

chapter 5

For Bethany and Hamilton, it was pretty much a perfect week. Every day, they went down to the warm sand, where Sam would play football, frisbee or cricket with Grandie. Sam had also made friends among the other boys who lived close by or who were visiting their families, and so he always had someone to play with.

Bethany, left to herself, would happily slip Hamilton out of her pocket so that they could build sandcastles together and make shell patterns in the sand. When the tide was out, they'd explore the rock pools. To Hamilton, they looked like small underwater countries, with forests of feathery seaweed and hillsides with shell houses made out of clinging limpets. Tiny fishes darted in and out among glowing sea anemones. It all looked so magical that Hamilton wished he could be a hamster-fish and swim in and out of the seaweed forests. As a Syrian hamster, however, Hamilton mustn't get wet, but back at Nan and Grandie's house, Bethany would tell him stories about a magic water hamster who lived under the sea and ran on a silver wheel. Hamilton, who loved aeroplanes, thought he'd rather be a flying hamster, but silver wheels were a nice idea, too.

Sometimes in the evenings, the family would get together to play a game, and Bethany would bring Hamilton down to watch. He found it all very interesting, but he could get thoroughly frustrated, too. If they played Scrabble, he could see great opportunities for words like 'gustation' (tasting something – Hamilton liked to do this if there were apples involved), 'ziffius' (a sea monster) and 'excogitate' (to work something out by thinking hard about it, which Hamilton also liked to do a lot). He had once read a story with a ziffius in it, and was pretty sure that they didn't really exist, but you never know. 'Apple' was a favourite word of his, too.

If they played a murder–mystery game, Hamilton knew who'd done it, how they did it, what with and why long before anybody else did. The quiz programmes on television were too easy, but sometimes there were programmes with exciting music, and one night there was a documentary all about aeroplanes, which Hamilton loved. He watched Grandie and Sam playing chess, too, and tried to guess the moves they would make next.

In Bethany's room, Hamilton and Bethany

would sort out the shells and pebbles they had picked up on the beach. There was always sand in Bethany's sandals and in her bag, and Hamilton would wriggle about in it, lifting it high and letting it trickle through his paws.

'You can't get enough of sand, can you, Hamilton?' said Bethany. He ran up her arm to rub his face against her hand and put out his paw for the phone.

LAST DAY 2MORO, he tapped out.

'I know,' said Bethany. 'So we'll make it a really good day. We'll spend every moment we can on the beach, all right? You'll have to stay awake all day, if you can. And we'll still have Saturday morning left, before we go home.'

Hamilton nodded sadly, ran into his cage and picked up the puzzle he'd been doing. Wherever you were, there was always Sudoku.

Hamilton did his puzzle and Bethany curled up with a book. But if they had looked out of the window, they might have seen a dark-haired young man with a black box in his hand walking slowly along the shore.

Tim was walking along the beach with the remote-control tracking device in his hand, watching to see if it lit up and listening for the quiet bleep that would tell him that his microspeck was nearby. This evening, he had walked up and down the main street in Kettle Bay and along the beach and there hadn't been as much as a flicker or a peep out of it. Finally, he returned to the Hammock and Spinnaker, where he banged his head on a low beam over the front door. It was a very old house, the oldest in the village, and had been built in the days when people were shorter than they are now. It had a stone floor, dark wooden furniture and a glowing log fire in the lounge. Lizzie the landlady greeted him.

'Did you enjoy your walk, Dr Taverner?' she asked cheerfully as she dried glasses.

'Oh, yes, thank you!' said Tim, but he hadn't really enjoyed it much. He hadn't noticed the pleasant sea air, the shells, the waves, the rock pools or the dogs barking at the sea. All he cared about was that microspeck and he had had no luck whatsoever. There was no sign of it.

'Can you call me at about seven in the morning?' he asked.

'Certainly, Dr Taverner!' said Lizzie.

Tim went back to his small bedroom with the flowered curtains at the little low window. This time he remembered to duck, scowling. The room wasn't made for six-foot-two computer scientists.

chapter 6

However careful you are about eating a picnic on the beach, you always get sand in the sandwiches. Bethany was thinking this as she sprawled on a rug in the sunshine, secretly slipping bits of sandwich into the sandcastle where Hamilton was hiding, nibbling them from her fingers. A piece of driftwood from the shoreline made a very good bridge across the moat and an excellent hiding place for Hamilton. He would rather have been out on the open sand, warming his fur in the sun – but

41

as Nan, Grandie and Sam were all there, it was safer to hide under the bridge.

Hamilton found a bit of driftwood that had broken from the bridge and gnawed it. Lolly sticks were good for chewing on while you made them into flags, but not as satisfying as driftwood. Just that morning, Bethany had given him a new flag, but he wouldn't dream of chewing that because she had made it specially for him. It had a picture of a golden hamster on a white background, and it was his newest treasure. He had it with him, hidden under the drawbridge. There was still a faint whiff of lemon about it, from when it had been a lemon ice lolly stick. Hamilton nibbled at the driftwood again – it was good for getting your teeth into, even if it could be a bit salty. He'd have to ask Bethany to take some home.

'Are you looking forward to seeing your rabbit again, Sam?' asked Nan.

'Suppose so,' said Sam. 'I'll take him some dandelions. I don't know why Bethany wanted to bring Hammy on holiday. He just sleeps in his cage in the house all day.'

'But you have him to come home to in the evenings, don't you, Bethany?' said Nan. 'He really is a sweetie.'

'*Sweetie*'? 'Hammy' was bad enough! Hamilton gave Bethany's finger a gentle nip, not enough to hurt, but enough to say that he objected. 'Sweetie' was a word for brightly coloured things that were bad for the teeth. He wasn't a humbug, a jelly bean or a pink-and-white marshmallow, was he? Why did people always say he was *sweet*?

Presently, Nan said she and Grandie were going back to the house, as she needed to sort out some washing and Grandie was hoping to watch the cricket. 'But you two can stay here, if you like,' she said. 'Shall I check on Hamilton for you, Bethany?'

'No, please don't,' said Bethany quickly, and looked away because she could feel her face turning pink. 'He doesn't like to be disturbed when he's sleepy, and it upsets him, so he gets hyperactive and bites. I wouldn't go near him just now, if I were you.'

Hamilton's head butted her hand and she giggled.

'What's funny?' asked Sam.

'Nothing,' she said. 'Just thinking about hyperactive hamsters, that's all. It's no problem, Nan, if you and Grandie go back. I've got my phone and we're only five minutes from the house.'

Bethany glanced around for Hamilton, but there was no sign of him. Their special pebble, however, lay on the surface near the sandcastle. She thought she could see the sand move as he wriggled underneath it. Sam had

wandered over to the rock pools to look for
hermit crabs.

Bethany left Hamilton to play and ran down
to the shoreline, letting the small tickling waves
run over her toes. Looking over her shoulder,
she could just about see Hamilton's pebble
beside the sandcastle. The waves teased at her
feet, and from the way they were moving
steadily up the shoreline she could tell that the
tide was coming in. By the evening, most of
the beach would be under water. She ran back
up the beach, picked up the pebble and
scrabbled in the sand with her hands.

'Hamilton?' she said. There was a shuffling in
the sand and Hamilton popped up. She held
out her hand and he climbed on to it.

'Hamilton, the tide's coming in,' she said,
stroking his back. 'Take care. Don't get wet.'

Hamilton put out his paw for the phone and
Bethany held it out to him.

I KNOW, he told her. I CHECKED TIDE TIMES
IN NEWSPAPER.

'All right, so you're a cleverclogs,' she said.
Hamilton tried to look modest and failed. 'But
you need to keep popping up so you can see
where you are – and so *I* can see where you
are, too. OK? Now, I'm going to finish my
castle.'

Hamilton popped into a tunnel and waved
the flag out at her. He loved that flag.

The castle needed more shells, pebbles and
seaweed, so Bethany was soon on her knees in
the sand, running it through her hands and
choosing the prettiest shells. While Bethany
decorated her castle, Hamilton did a bit of
tunnelling then scrabbled his way to the surface,
shook himself and rubbed his face with his
paws to clean off the sand. He scratched at each
ear in turn and shook his head. *There, that's*

better. He sniffed at the air and looked out to sea.

What Hamilton saw was very strange, and he needed a better look. For a moment, he thought he was looking at a real live ziffius, but that wasn't likely, was it? He ran a little nearer to the shore, taking care not to get his paws wet, and looked again.

It wasn't a ziffius, it was a boat – a long, thin boat – and the man sitting in it was using a paddle to propel it along. He didn't seem to be finding it easy. It looked as if he was trying to steer the boat towards the shore, but it didn't want to go. It lurched dangerously one way and then the other as if it wanted to throw the man out. Whenever it tipped to one side, the man leant the other way to balance it. Hamilton was sure this wasn't meant to happen. He should tell Bethany.

Hamilton ran across the sand and found

Bethany carefully placing a ring of cockle shells along a castle wall. He didn't like to disturb her, but this was important, so he climbed on to her lap and scratched at her hand with his paw. She smoothed his fur and gently stroked his paw, but she was concentrating on her castle and kept her eyes on the shells.

'Hello, Hamilton,' she said. 'Do you want to help? Are you going to choose a shell for me? You can be the king of this castle when it's finished.'

There was only one thing for Hamilton to do. He nipped her.

'Ow!' she said, and finally looked down. 'What was that for?'

Hamilton pointed out to sea with one paw and pulled at her thumb with the other, like a child pulling on its mother's hand.

Bethany shielded her eyes against the bright water, but it was still difficult to see clearly.

'There's a man in a canoe,' she said. 'What's he doing out there?' This wasn't a safe place for canoeing. Bethany remembered all she'd learnt about the strong and dangerous currents in the bay.

As she watched, the boat suddenly rocked. Bethany scrambled to her feet.

'Hamilton, he's capsized!'

chapter 7

Bethany dashed to the rocks, with Hamilton racing across the sand beside her. 'Sam!' she yelled as she tapped three 9s into her phone. 'Sam, look!'

Sam had been bending over a rock pool with his back to the sea. By the time he looked up, Hamilton had hidden behind a stone.

'Look, Sam!' Bethany shouted, pointing to the sea. 'There, in the water! Go and get Nan and Grandie.'

Sam dashed away as somebody from the

Emergency Services spoke to her. 'My name's Bethany Elliott . . . I'm at Kettle Bay and there's a man in the water . . . His canoe's turned over . . . Yes, there's a lifebelt here . . . If I can reach it . . . yes, I've got it! I don't know if I can throw it very far, but I'll try . . .' Bethany knew about lifebelts. She had been to a life-saving course after school and they had practised using lifebelts to pull each other across the hall floor, which was supposed to be the sea, but this was very different. She was sure she couldn't throw far enough, but she'd try her best.

'Don't panic!' she yelled, but she knew the man couldn't hear her from so far away. Hamilton popped up from behind the stone and came to stand beside her. 'I'll throw you a lifebelt!'

Battling against the waves and spitting out seawater, Tim had seen the girl on the shore with the lifebelt, and when he shook the water out of his eyes, he was pretty sure that she was the hamster girl. He hadn't come all this way, and come so close to that hamster, to give up the hunt now. He remembered his remote-control tracking device and tried to reach into the pocket of his shorts to get it out, but it had gone. It must be at the bottom of the sea by now.

Bethany flung the lifebelt as hard and as far as she could, but it still fell short of Tim, who didn't even seem to notice it at first. She shouted so hard that it hurt. 'Swim! Swim to the lifebelt!'

Splashing his way through the waves, Tim reached the lifebelt and struggled into it. Then, in a determined effort to find the tracker, he tried to duck under the water, but the lifebelt held him up. He couldn't believe it, he couldn't lose the tracker when he was so close to finding the hamster!

Bethany couldn't understand why the man still wasn't trying to swim for shore. He seemed to be looking for something all the way out there in the middle of the sea. 'Come *on!*' yelled Bethany encouragingly. 'Come on, *kick!* Kick your legs harder!'

Even Hamilton, who did not like water and had no intention of being in it, knew what the man should be doing. He came out from behind his stone and kicked his legs to show the man.

Tim Taverner squinted towards the shore. *Was that . . .?* No, it couldn't be . . . But right next to the girl's foot, there appeared to be the very hamster Tim had been looking for. With a fresh burst of energy, Tim kicked and paddled as hard as he could back towards the beach.

'That's it!' shouted Bethany. 'Now hold on tight!'

She was shouting so loudly and concentrating so hard that she hadn't noticed the sound of footsteps on the rocks behind her, but Hamilton had, and he'd hidden again. Then Grandie was behind her saying 'Well done, sweetheart!' and his big, strong hands were on the rope, helping her to haul the man to safety. Nan and Sam were running, too, carrying a blanket and towels, and soon there was the sound of an engine and the slamming of doors as two lifeguards arrived in their van and ran to the rocks. By the time they got there, however, Bethany and Grandie had hauled a soaked and bedraggled Tim Taverner to safety and were helping him out of the water.

Hamilton could see that everything would be all right now. A lot of people were arriving. It looked as though everyone was about to get very wet, including himself if he stayed there,

and besides, he didn't want to be seen. While
everybody gathered round the wet, shivery
man, Hamilton found a sunny patch of sand,
left the pebble there to mark it and hid
underneath.

Bethany, glancing over her shoulder to see
where he was, saw the pebble. *Sensible hamster*,
she thought as she held on to Tim's arm.

Water poured from Tim's hair and his
soaked clothes. It ran in chilly wet pathways
down the back of his neck, into his sandals
and into the crook of his cramped leg as the
lifeguards helped him to limp from the sea.
He shivered uncontrollably, and his teeth
chattered as they sat him down on the sand.
Three other children were on their way to the
beach – the two small boys stopped to see
what was going on, but an older girl told
them to stop staring and go and build a castle
instead.

Tim tried very hard to say 'hamster'. He had seen it – he knew he had! But between shivering and shock, all he could manage was 'H . . . h . . . h . . . h . . .', and Nan thought he was asking for help. She held his hand.

'It's all right now,' she soothed him. 'We're helping you. I'm Linda. Can you tell me your name?'

'T . . . Tim . . . T . . .' he began, and wished he hadn't, because he preferred to keep his name secret when he was spying on the hamster. A hamster that seemed to have somehow disappeared. Again. 'Tim Thompson,' he lied.

'Well, you're safe now, Tim,' she said. She hugged the blanket round him and rubbed his arms so vigorously that Bethany thought he'd catch fire.

Looking at him, Bethany had a feeling she'd met him before, but it was hard to tell. His hair was half dried and sticking up, his eyes were pink, and the ordeal had left his face puffy and bloated. He could have been anybody. She knelt down and took his free hand, warming it between both of hers.

'You're freezing,' she said. 'I'm sorry you lost your canoe, but at least you're all right. You've been very lucky.'

Tim supposed he should say thank you, but he couldn't quite manage the words. He didn't *feel* very lucky.

chapter 8

As Tim gathered the blanket round himself
and shuddered, Nan, Grandie and the
lifeguards discussed what to do with him.
The lifeguards were very keen to take him to
hospital in case he needed medical attention,
but Nan said the only attention he needed was
a hot bath and an even hotter drink. The
other children had stopped staring and were
running down the sand to paddle in the sea.
One of the lifeguards followed them, and
Bethany knew he'd be warning them about

the currents and pointing out what had
happened to Tim.

'You really should go to hospital, sir,' said one
of the lifeguards. 'They need to check you over.'

Tim was horribly cold and wet, and his eyes
were still stinging from the salt water, but in
spite of that, he tried to think clearly. The girl
on her knees rubbing warmth into his hand was
the girl from Tumblers Crescent! She was the
one who had brought her hamster on holiday,
and that hamster was probably the one with the
microchip! He hadn't made all this effort – and
nearly drowned – to be taken off to hospital
when the hamster was nearby.

'I . . . I . . . I'm f . . . f-f-fine,' he said, although
he was still shivering too much to speak clearly.
'If . . . if . . . L . . . L-Linda and . . .'

'Martin,' said Grandie. 'I'm Martin, and this
is our Bethany, who threw you the lifebelt, and
Sam, who came to get help.'

'Th . . . th-thank you very much,' said Tim. 'You're b-both . . .' He was thinking, *You're both coming between me and the hamster with MY microspeck!* But what he said was, 'You're b-both very brave. I really d . . . d-d-don't need to go to hospital, but I'd like to t-t-t-take you up on your offer, L-Linda, if it's no t-trouble.'

'We'll have a hot bath ready for you in five minutes,' said Nan.

The lifeguards helped Tim across the dunes and into their van to drive him to Nan and Grandie's house. They offered Sam a lift, too, and let him try on their life-jackets while he asked Tim what it was like to fall out of a canoe. Bethany hung back.

'Aren't you coming, Bethany?' asked Nan.

'I'll be up in a minute,' she said, adding truthfully, 'I've left some shells on the beach.' The real reason, of course, was that she had to go back for Hamilton, who had been alone for quite long enough. She didn't know how long they'd been sitting there with the dripping-wet canoeist, but the other three children had now finished building their castle and were trailing back up through the sand dunes, saying something about ice creams.

Bethany ran down to the place where Hamilton had last left the pebble, rubbing her arms and realizing too late that she had forgotten her cardigan. The incoming tide was bringing a breeze with it, and the afternoon was turning cooler.

She was pretty certain of the right spot, but when she reached it, there was no sign at all of the pebble. Hamilton must have moved it. She walked carefully, her eyes on the sand, watching for any sign of the pebble – or of Hamilton.

The gleam of a pebble caught her eye – no, that wasn't the one. There was something moving on the sand . . . but it was just a crab running sideways across the beach. Bethany began to be afraid. Among all the pebbles on the beach, there was not a trace of Hamilton's marker stone. Perhaps the sand had covered it – Bethany curled her toes, but there was still no pebble. She was looking down so intently that she hardly noticed the sandcastle until she'd nearly stepped on it.

It wasn't one of her castles – the other children must have made it. Stones, shells and seaweed formed a pattern over it, and there, in the middle of a swirl of shells and pebbles, was Hamilton's stone. Bethany snatched it up in relief and plunged her hand into the sandcastle. Hamilton loved sandcastles, so he must have moved into this one!

'Hello, Hamilton!' she said. 'Are you in there?'

There was no welcoming wriggle of warm fur against her hand, and no moving of the sand under her fingers. Perhaps he was fast asleep, but she bit her lip with anxiety.

'Hamilton?' she said, pushing her hands further into the sand. 'Are you in there?'

The waves rippled further up the beach. Bethany felt hot, then cold, and panic made her hands shake. Where was he? And why had she found the pebble, and not Hamilton?

Then she understood. The children building the sandcastle must have found it and put it there, and she was cross with herself for not realizing that straight away. With each new wave, the sea crept further up the beach, and the need to find Hamilton grew more urgent. She stood up and turned slowly, scanning the beach. It was a small, enclosed bay, but it was still a vast wilderness for a small hamster, who could be anywhere.

Watching the sand for movement, she ran, but then it occurred to her that she might step on Hamilton or fall over him. After that, Bethany walked quickly instead and as lightly as she could. Nobody was about, so she called his name: 'Hamilton? Can you hear me? I'm here, I'm trying to find you. If you can hear me, come to me! *Stay away from the water!*'

Step by step, Bethany worked her way up the beach, curling her fingers tightly as she called his name. She straightened up, rubbing her arms. It was cold now. Sooner or later somebody would come looking for her and call her in for tea, and she didn't know what she'd say. She couldn't leave without Hamilton. Bethany tiptoed further, sometimes sinking to her knees and crawling, feeling the sand with her fingers as she called Hamilton's name and tried to guess where he might have gone. He was intelligent, and he knew that the tide was coming in. He'd probably get as high up the beach as he could, somewhere the tide would never reach . . . He'd have gone to the sand dunes!

Bethany broke into a run, forgetting to take care where she put her feet, until she nearly stepped on a blade of sharp, spiky grass and wobbled, with one foot still in mid-air. As she found her balance again, a tiny flash of colour caught her attention.

She knelt carefully to examine the sand, and this time she saw it clearly.

It was a tiny flag, made from a lolly stick. On the top, very tattered and crumpled by now, was a sweet wrapper with a picture of a golden hamster on its hind legs.

'Hamilton!' she cried. 'You're here!'

She plunged her hands into the sand. This time, the sand was warm, and with a happy flood of relief she felt the soft wriggling of Hamilton's thick fur under her fingers. Two ears appeared out of the sand, then Hamilton's bright face and happy eyes as he jumped on to her lap, and she laughed with joy and relief.

'Are you cold?' she asked, cuddling him gently. 'Poor Hamilton! Were you frightened?'

Hamilton shook his head energetically and rubbed his face against her hand, but really he had been a bit scared, and was as glad to see Bethany as she was to find him. When the children had taken his pebble, he had tunnelled under the sand, wanting to put himself as near to the pebble as possible so that Bethany could easily find him. As he got closer to it, though, he had decided that it was a bad idea. He would be in great danger of being found by the other children, who would call him Fluffpot and Sweetie and might even take him home, and Bethany would never know what had happened to him. That thought was utterly terrifying. Faced with the double danger of the new children and the waves creeping up the beach, Hamilton had tunnelled furiously towards the dunes to get as far away from the sea as he could. Then he had stopped tunnelling when he remembered that Bethany would have no way of finding him. He had turned himself about, run to Bethany's castle, collected his flag and carried it in his teeth to the safety of the dunes. Once there, he had planted it as a marker, then curled up and hid, finally snoozing lightly underneath it. He was blissfully thankful to settle into the warmth of Bethany's hands at last.

'Time to go home and get warm,' she said. 'You need your warm cosy nest. Now, Hamilton, you need to know that we've got a visitor at home – that man from the canoe. His name's Tim, and Nan and Grandie have brought him home to look after him. They don't know that I brought you here with me, so I have to slip you back carefully.'

Hamilton nodded and put a claw to his lips. He'd be very good. He'd go straight into his cage, curl up and be no trouble at all. Excitement was tiring, and he'd had enough for one day.

chapter 9

Tim Taverner was perhaps the most brilliant scientist ever to work at the town's university, but wrapped in Grandie's dressing gown, he didn't look or feel clever at all.

Nan and Grandie were taking such care of him that he'd hardly been let out of their sight. Nan had run him a hot bath, but she said that he was still in a state of shock and might faint while he was in there, so he mustn't lock the bathroom door in case he collapsed and needed first aid. Grandie sat outside on the stairs, ready to run to Tim's rescue if he heard anything alarming that might mean Tim had fallen over. Fortunately, nothing of the kind happened. Tim didn't need rescuing, and he felt a lot better for that hot bath. Nan had washed his clothes and put them in the tumble dryer, and left him Grandie's dressing gown and slippers.

Emerging from the bathroom, red in the face from the heat, Tim caught sight of a half-open door across the landing. Through it, he glimpsed books, a sketch book, pencils, a floppy cuddly dog and a mauve dressing gown over the back of the door. That had to be Bethany's room, and the hamster must be in there! His heart beat faster with excitement. Was anybody watching? He glanced over his shoulder.

'You look better for that!' said Grandie, smiling broadly and striding towards him.

'Kettle's on. Come downstairs. The sitting room's this way.'

There was no escape. With his glasses misting up, Tim meekly followed Grandie downstairs.

'Where are you staying, Tim?' asked Nan as she poured the tea.

'I have a room at the Hamster and Spinacher,' said Tim, who was still thinking about his microspeck. 'I mean, the Sandwich and Hammocker . . .'

'Oh, you mean the Hammock and Spinnaker,' she corrected him. 'When you've warmed up and your clothes are dry, we'll take you back there. Don't you have any shoes?'

Tim's sandals had come off while he was in the water, and Grandie's shoes wouldn't fit him. Nan offered to phone the Hammock and Spinnaker and ask to have his shoes brought round, but Tim said that he had caused enough trouble already and wouldn't hear of it. It was really that he didn't want anyone calling the Hammock and Spinnaker asking for 'Dr Thompson's' shoes, because he had booked the room under his real name, Dr Taverner, and Lizzie the landlady wouldn't know anything about a Dr Thompson.

'I'll go home in bare feet,' he said hastily. 'I don't mind, really.'

'Well, you can get those feet warm by our fire first,' said Nan firmly. 'It scares me to think what might have happened to you. You've had a very lucky escape. I don't know what might have happened if our Bethany and Sam hadn't been there.'

'Yes, Bethany,' he replied eagerly, 'I really need to thank her very much. Where is she?'

'She's out,' said Nan. 'I expect she'll be home soon.'

Good, thought Tim, who presumed Nan meant Bethany had come back from the beach and gone out again. *I can steal the hamster while she's out of the way.* Then he had what seemed to him like a very good idea. 'Perhaps I could write her a thank you note!' he said. 'I could leave it in her room for her.'

He imagined himself writing the note and leaving it in Bethany's room. While he was in there, he would find the hamster cage – it was bound to be there somewhere – grab the animal, and get it out of the house without anyone knowing. That bit might be difficult. If he could go back wearing Grandie's dressing gown, he could put the hamster in the pocket. His own clothes might by dry by then, and he wasn't sure he could fit a hamster into the pocket of his shorts or hide it under his T-shirt. Perhaps if he shivered or coughed, they would lend him the dressing gown until he got his own clothes back. Yes, that was the best way. He shivered and coughed convincingly.

'A thank you note!' said Nan. 'What a nice idea! I'll bring you some paper and a pen.' When Tim had started to write, she added, 'But there's no need to take it upstairs. You're still shivery, and now you've got a cough. We'll just leave your note here on the mantelpiece and Bethany will see it as soon as she gets home. Oh, here's our Sam! Sam, come and keep Tim company! You can tell him all about your holiday. And your rabbit. And tell Tim about all those computer games you play, because I'm sure he'll understand them far better than I do.'

Tim sighed deeply but managed to turn it into a yawn. He closed his eyes and wondered if he'd ever get his hands on that hamster. Sam sat down on the floor beside him.

'Hi!' he said. 'Which one shall I talk about first?'

★

Bethany hurried home, Hamilton safe in the bag over her shoulder next to a few shells and pebbles and a handful of sand. She kept her hand over him, partly to keep him warm, but also just so that she could feel he was safe. After all her worry about him, it was so precious to feel the warm rise and fall of his breathing and the little pattering beat of his heart. Nan had left the back door unlocked for her, and, not wanting to disturb Hamilton, she left her sandals outside and slipped into the house as quietly as possible.

'There you are!' said Nan, who was taking something made of lycra from the tumble dryer. 'Dr Thompson's in the sitting room. He wanted to say thank you.'

Bethany ran upstairs first, placed Hamilton gently in his nest box and covered him up to keep him warm, then went to the sitting room to meet Dr Thompson. But looking round the door, she saw Sam seated on the floor talking to Tim, who was fast asleep next to the fire with his mouth open. It would be a shame to wake him, so she left without a sound.

Sam had been very helpful, keeping Tim company. He had chatted about cricket, rock pools, rabbits and reaching Level Five on Fantasy Koala Quest, while Tim had leant back in his chair, closed his eyes and pretended to listen. Suddenly he felt very tired. Soon he was dreaming of swimming round and round a rock pool with a rabbit, while a koala with a cricket bat paddled his canoe out to sea. He was still dreaming when Nan came in.

'Bless him,' she said softly. 'All that excitement and then a comfy chair near the fire, of course he's fallen asleep. It seems a real pity to disturb him, but I think he should be in his bed at the Hammock and Spinnaker. His clothes are dry now, so I'll take him back there.'

She shook Tim gently by the shoulder. 'Dr Thompson!'

Tim woke up with a shout, because in his dream the rabbit was trying to drown him. Bethany wandered upstairs to check that Hamilton hadn't been scared by the noise. She was still there when Tim, with bare feet and wearing his canoeing kit under Grandie's dressing gown, was bundled into Nan and Grandie's car and driven back to the Hammock and Spinnaker.

'Our Bethany will be sad to have missed you,' said Nan, 'but I'll make sure she gets your note.'

'Oh, yes, and please say thank you from me,' said Tim, remembering at last that Bethany had, after all, saved his life while he was trying to steal her hamster. He ought to try to see her. There was still tomorrow.

Back at the Hammock and Spinnaker, he relived the scene at the bay – the way he had lost control of the canoe, how it had tipped one way, and then tipped the other way, and then finally tipped him into the freezing sea. He saw again the child throwing the lifebelt . . .

There had definitely been something beside her – something hamster-like, he was sure of it. It wasn't just the freezing cold water that was making him imagine things, was it?

Lizzie the landlady brought him a cup of tea. 'Are you feeling better now?' she asked. 'Everybody's heard about your little adventure today. Didn't you have a life-jacket? Now drink that while it's hot. That's a nice dressing gown you've got on.'

Tim smiled to himself. It was Bethany's grandfather's. That meant he'd have to take it back to the house tomorrow. One more chance.

chapter 10

The next morning was bright and sunny, and Bethany woke up looking forward to one last visit to the beach. Hamilton was already standing on the windowsill, with his paws on the glass and his nose twitching. He turned towards her, his eyes shining, and pointed hopefully towards the sandy beach.

'That's what I want to do, too,' she said. 'It's our last morning. Grandie's taking us home later today, but I don't suppose he'll want to go just yet.'

Hamilton ran to the door, squeezed underneath it and scurried along the landing to stand at the door of Nan and Grandie's room. He didn't even need to go in to hear what sounded like a motorbike engine but which was only Grandie snoring. How could anyone sleep through that? He shook his head in disapproval, slipped under the door and, out of kindness to Nan, tickled Grandie under the chin (taking good care not to get too close to that snorting mouth). As he had hoped, the tickle made Grandie's mouth close (Hamilton got even further out of the way when that was happening), and the snoring stopped. Hamilton ran back to Bethany and put his head to one side on his paws to show that Nan and Grandie were asleep.

'If they're not even up yet, there's plenty of time,' said Bethany, and she jumped out of bed to get dressed. 'Hamilton, don't you dare go one inch out of my sight. I've had quite enough scares for one holiday.'

This time, Bethany remembered her cardigan, and Hamilton refused to go in her shoulder bag as he preferred to sit in her pocket, from where he could look out. Down on the beach there was time for one more castle, with a bridge, battlements and flags at every corner, and they wrote, 'GOODBYE, KETTLE BAY' in big letters in the sand. When an aeroplane roared overhead, Hamilton gazed up until he fell over backwards, and he lay looking at the sky and wondering why all his favourite things were happening at once. He tried writing his own name by running through the sand to make furrows and leaping from one letter to another to keep them from joining together. It wasn't very clear as the sand kept trickling back into the letters as soon as they were made, but he was pleased with it.

'I don't want to go home,' sighed Bethany. 'I love it here. I wish we could stay.'

Hamilton tipped up her bag so that her phone fell out (which, for hamster paws, was a lot easier than dragging the phone out). He opened the phone book, found her home number and pointed to it.

'You want me to phone Mum and Dad?' she said, puzzled. Hamilton shook his head, put his paws on where his hips should be and wrinkled up his nose at her.

'Oh, you mean I'll see Mum and Dad soon,' she said. 'Yes, I suppose that'll be nice.' He took the phone back and showed her another name in the phone book.

'Chloe,' she read. 'Yes, I've missed Chloe. I'll see how Toffee's doing, and I've collected some shells for her. It'll be fun to give them to her.'

U'LL HAVE YR OWN ROOM AGAIN, he texted.

82

After a little thought, he added, CAN WE COME
HERE AGAIN?

'Oh, Hamilton, of course we can! We'll be
back soon!' she said, and picked him up, but he
wriggled to be down again. He was very fond
of Bethany, but she would always be there. The
beach was a treat to be enjoyed while he could.
By the time he'd explored the sandcastle, run
round the moat in circles and chewed the
drawbridge into shreds, more people were
coming to the beach, some with dogs to walk,
and Bethany decided it was time to take
Hamilton home.

Later that morning, Tim Taverner called at Nan
and Grandie's house with Grandie's dressing
gown, a bunch of flowers and a gift-wrapped
box of chocolates. He looked a lot smarter and
more impressive than he had the day before.

'Hello again!' he said as Nan opened the

door. 'I didn't get to say thank you to Bethany properly yesterday, so I've brought her some flowers and a present.'

'How lovely!' said Nan. 'But I'm afraid you've just missed her. What a shame!'

'Oh!' gasped Tim. 'Oh! Yes, that is a shame!'

He looked so disappointed that Nan felt very sorry for him. 'Martin just took Bethany and Sam home,' she said, and in the hope of making him feel better, added, '– they didn't want to go. They'd had a lovely time.'

Tim couldn't quite believe it. Why was that hamster always one step ahead of him?

'Oh . . . I . . . I . . . ,' he stammered, 'I so wanted to meet her.'

'If you'd been twenty minutes earlier, you'd have caught her,' she said, which made it worse for poor Tim. 'Off they went with their collections of shells – and Bethany's hamster. She insisted on bringing it!'

'Hamster,' repeated Tim weakly.

'Yes, she won't be parted from it,' said Nan. 'I'm so sorry you missed her, but I'll see her again soon. I'll take her the present.'

'The flowers won't last,' he said lamely, then added, 'so perhaps you'd like them, to say thank you for looking after me.'

'Oh, you sweetie!' she said, and kissed him on the cheek. 'Would you like to come in for a coffee?'

But Tim didn't want to stay at Kettle Bay a moment longer.

Back at home, Bethany put Hamilton's cage back in its place and opened the door. Hamilton woke up, let himself out and jumped on to the bed.

Now that she was home, Bethany found that it felt good to be there, with her own bed and her own things around her. Hamilton, who was bouncing on her bed, seemed to be glad too. He suddenly stopped bouncing, tapped her hand and put his paws over his eyes.

'What's the matter?' she asked.

He shook his head, pointed at her and did it again.

'Oh, you want *me* to hide my eyes?' she said. 'OK.'

She covered her face and listened. There was a bit of scuffling and clattering from the cage, then the click of keys on her phone and a gentle scratch on her arm to tell her she could look. Laid out in a row was her phone with the message PRESENT 4 U, their special pebble and a very battered lolly-stick flag with a picture of a hamster.

'Hamilton, what perfect presents!' she cried. 'And I've brought back a present for you, too.'

She placed a paper bag on the floor, and

Hamilton climbed down to it and wriggled himself inside. First, he pulled out a bit of driftwood and chewed it. *Oh, that is good!* It tasted of the seaside, and the texture was perfect, too.

'There's something else in there,' said Bethany. Hamilton looked again – and this time he hurled himself into the bag, ripping it open in his enthusiasm as he rolled over and over in the most wonderful present – lovely, light, soft, swishy, swirly *SAND*!

It all started with a Scarecrow

Puffin is well over sixty years old.
Sounds ancient, doesn't it? But Puffin has never been
so lively. We're always on the lookout for the next big
idea, which is how it began all those years ago.

Penguin Books was a big idea from the mind of
a man called Allen Lane, who in 1935 invented
the quality paperback and changed the world.
**And from great Penguins, great Puffins grew,
changing the face of children's books forever.**

The first four Puffin Picture Books were hatched in 1940 and the
first Puffin story book featured a man with broomstick arms called
Worzel Gummidge. In 1967 Kaye Webb, Puffin Editor, started the
Puffin Club, promising to **'make children into readers'**.
She kept that promise and over 200,000 children became
devoted Puffineers through their quarterly instalments of
Puffin Post, which is now back for a new generation.

Many years from now, we hope you'll look back and
remember Puffin with a smile. **No matter what your age
or what you're into, there's a Puffin for everyone.**
The possibilities are endless, but one thing is for sure:
whether it's a picture book or a paperback, a sticker book
or a hardback, **if it's got that little Puffin
on it – it's bound to be good.**